Counting
Cows

For Ava – *D.S.*
For Sarah – *W.S.*

A Red Fox Book

Published by Random House Children's Books
20 Vauxhall Bridge Road, London SW1V 2SA

A division of The Random House Group Ltd
London Melbourne Sydney Auckland
Johannesburg and agencies throughout the world

1 3 5 7 9 10 8 6 4 2

First published in Great Britain by
Hutchinson Children's Books, 1994
Red Fox edition 2000

Printed in Singapore by Tien Wah Press (PTE) Ltd

THE RANDOM HOUSE GROUP Limited Reg. No. 954009

www.randomhouse.co.uk

ISBN 0 09 176467 X

Counting Cows

Dyan Sheldon
and Wendy Smith

RED
FOX

Dara can't sleep.

'When I can't sleep, I count sheep,' says Dara's father.
　'I don't want to count sheep,' says Dara.
　Her father looks at her. 'Why not?' he asks.

'Because I don't like sheep,' says Dara. 'I like cows.'
'Count cows then,' says Dara's father.
Dara frowns. 'But what colour are the cows?'
'Shut your eyes,' says Dara's father.

'Ready now?' Dara's father leans back in his chair. 'Imagine it's a sunny day. A herd of brown cows is standing in a large green field. There's a fence around the field. The cows start to move towards the fence. One by one they begin to jump. Count them slowly, Dara. One … two … three …'

'What's wrong?' asks her father. 'Aren't the brown cows moving?'

'Oh, the brown cows are moving all right,' says Dara. 'But the black-and-white cow is just lying on her side, gazing up at the sky.'

'She's doing what?' asks Dara's father.

'I think she must be counting the clouds in the sky,' says Dara.

'Let's begin again, shall we?' Dara's father makes himself comfortable. 'Close your eyes,' he says. 'Tell me what you see.'

Dara tells him. 'I see a sunny day. I see a big green field. There's a fence around the field. I see a herd of cows. All of the cows are brown except the one that's black and white.'

'And is the black-and-white cow moving?'

'Oh, yes,' says Dara. 'She's moving.'
  'Well that's good,' says Dara's father.
  'She's dancing around the field.'
  'Dancing around the field?'
  Dara smiles. 'Yes,' she says. 'I think it must be
because the butterflies are tickling her so much.'

'Now look here,' says Dara's father sternly. 'It's getting late. No more of this gazing at the clouds nonsense. No more being tickled by butterflies. Let's get ALL the cows over to the fence.'

'I'll try,' says Dara. She closes her eyes.

'What's happening?' asks her father.

'The cows are going to the fence.'

'Even the black-and-white cow?' asks her father.

'Oh, yes,' says Dara. 'Of course she is. That's where the best flowers are.'

Dara's father opens one eye. 'What flowers?'

'The flowers that my cow is picking,' says Dara.

'Picking?' repeats Dara's father. 'Cows can't pick flowers.'

'My cow can,' says Dara. 'She's picking them to put on her hat.'

'Shall we start again?' Dara's father leans back in his chair
and makes himself very very comfortable. 'Shut your eyes.'

Dara's eyes shut tight.

'Right,' says Dara's father. 'Your cow looks up and she sees
the cows all running across the field. Is she looking up, Dara?'

'She's looking up.'

'But not at the clouds,' says Dara's father. 'Or the butterflies. She stops picking flowers. She starts to run.'

'You're right!' cries Dara. 'She is starting to run.'

'She's running to the fence!' shouts Dara's father.

'No, she's not,' says Dara. 'She's running to the tub.'

Dara's father's eyes snap open. 'What tub? There isn't any tub in this field.'

'There is in my field,' says Dara. 'And my cow's taking a bath in it.'

'A bath?'

'She's very hot,' explains Dara. 'Because it's such a sunny day. And such a very big field.'

'Cows don't take baths,' says Dara's father.

'My cow loves to bathe,' says Dara. 'She likes the bubbles best.'

'I'm closing my eyes,' says Dara.

'Good,' says her father. 'And do you see the field? Do you see the cows?'

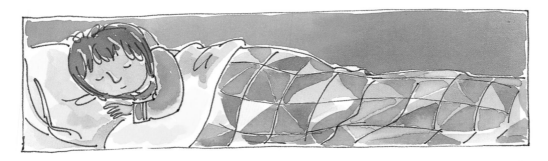

'Yes, I do,' says Dara. 'I see the cows and they're in the field.'

'And what are they doing?'
'They're watching my cow.'

'Because she's getting ready to jump over the fence?' asks Dara's father. He sounds hopeful.

'No,' says Dara, 'because she's swinging.'

Dara's father looks at Dara. 'She's swinging?'

'From a very big tree,' says Dara. 'She's drying herself off.'

Dara giggles. 'She forgot to bring a towel.'

Dara's father rubs his eyes. 'Perhaps if your cow is dry now, we could try just one more time.'

'All right,' says Dara. She closes her eyes.

'All set?'

'All set,' says Dara.

'Your cow has finished drying. She sees that the other cows are waiting for her. They know that she's the best jumper. They won't jump over the fence unless she goes first.'

'I see them!' says Dara. 'They're all in a line. They're waiting to go.'

'And your cow doesn't want to hold them up,' says Dara's father.

'She's trotting across the field. Faster and faster …

Closer and closer …

Can you see her, Dara? Can you see her getting ready to jump?'
Dara says, 'No.'

'No?' Dara's father opens his eyes.

Dara opens her eyes. 'No.'

'What do you mean "No"? Why isn't she getting ready to jump?'

'Because she's looking over the fence,' says Dara.

'At what?'

'At the ground,' says Dara.

'Whatever for?' asks Dara's father.

'In case it's too far away,' says Dara.

'She's not jumping off a cliff, you know,' says Dara's father. 'She's just jumping over a fence. Now close your eyes and really try to concentrate this time.'

'Your cow is finally getting ready to jump,' says Dara's father.
'She's galloping across the field. The other cows are following
her. Your cow picks up speed … She leaps into the air …
Can you see her, Dara? Can you see her leaping?'

Dara's eyes are closed. She sees her cow. Her cow is
galloping … The other cows are right behind her …
Dara's cow leaps into the air …

    Dara's father begins to count softly.

'One ...' he says.
'One ...' says Dara.

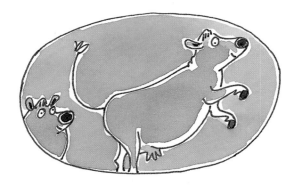

'Two ...' he says.
'Two ...' says Dara.

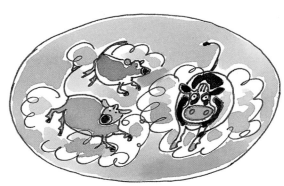

'Three ...' he says.
'Three ...' says Dara.

'Zzzz ...' he snores.
'Four ...' says Dara.
She tiptoes to the window.

'Five … six … seven … eight … nine ….'